GRRR!

Also available from Macmillan Children's Books

Wild!
Rhymes That Roar
Chosen by James Carter and Graham Denton

Journey to the Centre of My Brain
Poems by James Carter

Time-Travelling Underpants
Poems by James Carter

Greetings, Earthlings!
Space poems by
Brian Moses and James Carter

GRRR!

DINOS, DRAGONS & OTHER BEASTIE POEMS

JAMES CARTER &
GRAHAM DENTON

Illustrated by Chris Garbutt

MACMILLAN CHILDREN'S BOOKS

For Helen Fairlie, a grrreat editor
and a grrreat frrriend! (JC)

In memory of the late, grrreat Jeff Moss
(1942–1998) – always an inspiration. (GD)

First published 2013 by Macmillan Children's Books
a division of Macmillan Publishers Limited
20 New Wharf Road, London N1 9RR
Basingstoke and Oxford
Associated companies throughout the world
www.panmacmillan.com

ISBN 978-1-4472-2034-3

1 3 5 7 9 8 6 4 2

A CIP catalogue record for this book is available from the British Library.

Printed and bound by CPI Group (UK) Ltd, Croydon CR0 4YY

Contents

GRRReetings!

JAMES CARTER is crazy for crusty old critters. That's why, at least twice a year, he pops down to the Natural History Museum in Oxford, where he spends hours gawping at those old beasties, from the stuffed dodo bird to the megalosaurus bones to the towering iguanodon and T-rex skeletons. He'll then leave with his skull brimful with beastly ideas, many of which have gradually grown into full-size poems and have finally stomped and stamped their way into this book!

When **GRAHAM DENTON** was a little schoolboy he wasn't, well . . . exactly little! Being bigger and taller (and much, much stronger!) than all his classmates, he got the nickname 'Dino', after the dinosaur in the cartoon series *The Flintstones*, and the name stuck. Because of that, Graham had an affinity with dinosaurs from a very early age. He still owns an album of Brooke Bond PG Tips 'Dinosaur' cards that he collected nearly forty years ago. Graham continues to be fascinated by dinosaurs (and dragons and other deadly beasts too) and really enjoyed writing the poems for this book. And although he's never met a living dinosaur, he remains ever hopeful.

James and Graham bid you GRRReetings, readers, but advise you to b-b-beware, as beyond this page are the grrruesomist grrrumpsters and the beastliest beasties anywhere . . . all with plenty of GRRR! Don't say we didn't warn you!

Advice for a Dinosaur Spotter

Never say GRRR!
to a dinosaur
never you stamp
on its feet

Never you steal
a dinosaur egg
or hastily
beat a retreat

Never you stomp
on a dinosaur tail
never you jump
on its back

So all I can say
is keep out its way
or you'll be
a dinosaur snack!

James Carter

What Vexes T-rexes?

You know what really vexes
Tyrannosaurus rexes?

What makes us most unhappy
and very, very snappy?

When anybody calls us
T-rex – it truly galls us.

You see, that's not our full name.
And T-rex? What a *dull* name!

We're terrifying lizards
that rip out guts and gizzards;

our reputation's vital;
we need our proper title!

So *don't* abbreviate it.
We don't appreciate it.

There is no *T* before us –
the name's . . . *Tyrannosaurus*!

Graham Denton

Carnivore Alert!

Standing upright on two feet?
Carnivore alert!
Chomping on a chunk of meat?
Carnivore alert!

Muscles that he loves to flex?
(Look at those impressive pecs!)
Going by the name of Rex?
Carnivore alert!

Always spoiling for a fight?
Carnivore alert!
One enormous appetite?
Carnivore alert!

Knife-like teeth and long, sharp claws?
Block your ears up when he roars?
Watch out all you HERBIVORES . . .
Carnivore alert!

Graham Denton

Silly Question!

What do
you call
a
dinosaur
with jagged
teeth
and pointy
claws,
who's BIG
and M E A N
and full
of *Grrr*?

Why, silly you . . .
you call it 'Sir'!

(Duh!!!)

Graham Denton

What Are Dinos Made of?

Grr! Grr! Grr!
Grr!Grr!Grr!
Grr!
Grr!Grr!
Grr!
Grr!
Grr!
Grr!
Grr!
Grr!   Grr!   Grr!
Grr!Grr!Grr!Grr!
Grr!   Grr!   Grr!
Grr!Grr!
Grr!Grr!Grr!
Grr!Grr!Grr!Grr!
Grr!Grr!Grr!Grr!Grr!   Grr!
Grr!Grr!Grr!Grr!   Grr!   Grr!
Grr!   Grr!   Grr!   Grr!
Grr!   Grr!   Grr!
Grr!   Grr!
Grr!   Grr!
Grr!Grr!   Grr!Grr!

James Carter

5

Dinosaur Sounds

Did they *snort* like a rhino?
Did they *bellow* like a bull?
Did they *whinny* like a zebra?
Did they *scream* like a gull?
Did they *whine* like a mozzie?
Did they *neigh* like a mare?
Did they *yowl* like a jackal?
Did they *growl* like a bear?

Did they *shriek* like a peacock?
Did they *screech* like an owl?
Did they *whoop* like a monkey?
Did they *hoot*, did they *howl*?
Did they *click* like a dolphin?
Did they *cluck* like a hen?
Did they *chant* like a falcon?
Did they *warble* like a wren?

Did they *chirp* like an ostrich?
Did they *purr* like a cat?
Did they *crow* like a rooster?
Did they *squeal* like a rat?
Did they *cackle* like a chicken?
Did they *holler* like a moose?
Did they *creak* like a cricket?
Did they *honk* like a goose?

Did they *bark* like a dingo?
Did they *arf* like a dog?
Did they *trumpet* like an elephant?
Or *grunt* like a hog?
Well, whatever sounds came out of them
the one thing that's for sure –
there'd be no peace and quiet
with a DINOSAUR next door!

Graham Denton

Giganotosaurus

The largest of the carnivores,
giganotosaurus ate
as many little dinosaurs
would fit upon his plate.

In every passing pal he spied
a gastronomic treat –
his massive jaws he'd open wide
and grab a bite to eat.

He gobbled all their body parts
(he didn't like to waste).
He guzzled livers, kidneys, hearts
(he didn't have much taste).

His habits being unrefined,
no friends would come to dinner;
an invitation out to dine
meant ending up much thinner!

For nothing could quite satiate
this appetite for flesh –
giganotosaurus ate and ate,
and much preferred it fresh.

For were that meat completely rare
he swallowed it with relish.
He didn't go for fancy fare;
no meal would he embellish.

He loved it bloody, red and raw,
he wolfed it by the bucket –
he might have liked it even more
if he had thought to cook it!

Graham Denton

Dinosaur Footprints

Dinosaur footprints,
what can they tell us?
Dinosaur footprints,
what do they say?
Whether they walked
on two legs or four legs;
whether they stalked
their dinosaur prey;
whether their gait
was narrow or sprawling;
whether their pace
was rapid or slow;
whether their stride
was ever so wide;
whether they wiggled
their dinosaur toes!

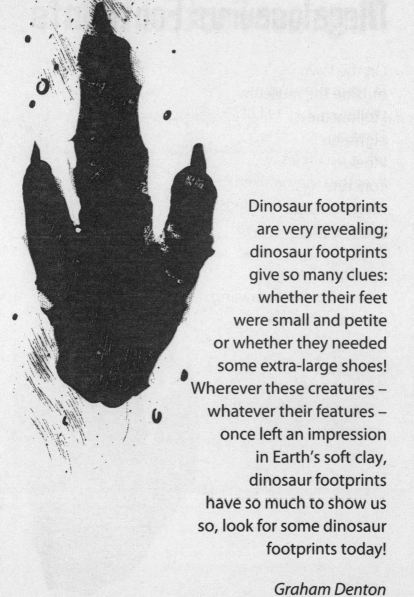

Dinosaur footprints
are very revealing;
dinosaur footprints
give so many clues:
whether their feet
were small and petite
or whether they needed
some extra-large shoes!
Wherever these creatures –
whatever their features –
once left an impression
in Earth's soft clay,
dinosaur footprints
have so much to show us
so, look for some dinosaur
footprints today!

Graham Denton

Megalosaurus Footprints

On the lawn
outside the museum
I follow the
eighteen
life-size
concrete
megalosaurus
footprints.

As I do
I realize
these prints are
bigger than both
my feet
put together,
and I estimate
that this great lizard
would have stood
six times my height,
moved four times
my speed
and devoured me
twice as quick
as I could scoff
any snack.

So . . .
  how come
    I'm here
      and he's
        not?

James Carter

Tyrannosaurus Sue

My name's Tyrannosaurus Sue,
come marvel at my fossil:
the *largest* T-rex skeleton,
I truly am colossal.
In all the world, the best-preserved,
the biggest, most complete;
my reputation's well deserved –
no other can compete.

My name's Tyrannosaurus Sue,
I'm really quite amazing,
I promise that you'll struggle to
avert your eyes from gazing.
A dinosaur with rex-appeal,
I live in this museum,
my bones each day upon display
where people flock to see 'um.

The queen of all the carnivores!
A prehistoric treasure!
I'm here for you to come and view –
peruse me at your leisure.
Oh yes, in your entire life
I guarantee that you
will *never* see a dino like
Tyrannosaurus Sue!

Graham Denton

'Tyrannosaurus Sue' is the largest, most extensive and best-
preserved *Tyrannosaurus rex* specimen ever found. She was
named after Sue Hendrickson, the fossil hunter who discovered
the skeleton in August 1990 in South Dakota, USA. Sue stands
4 metres tall (at the hip), is 12.3 metres long, and is a staggering
65 million years old. Over 200 of Sue's bones were preserved. The
skeleton includes the most complete T-rex tail, as well as one of
only two T-rex arms, ever found, and is considered one of the
most important fossil finds ever made. She's housed at the Field
Museum of Natural History in Chicago, Illinois, USA.

Night Thoughts of a T-rex Skeleton

The general public. You should see 'em,
crowding into MY museum:
poking, prodding at my bones.
Pesky humans, please go home!

If only I could live once more –
I'd let out one almighty roarrrrr,
then squish you all into the floor:
respect a long-dead dinosaur!

James Carter

Micropachycephalosaurus

This dino's in the hall of fame . . .
This dino's got the longest name!

Graham Denton

Strangely, despite the length of its name,
micropachycephalosaurus – meaning 'tiny thick-headed lizard' –
was actually one of the smallest dinosaurs, measuring in at only
0.5 to 1 metre in length. And if you want to know the dinosaur
with the shortest name . . . well, that honour goes to the minmi, a
3-metre-long armoured ankylosaur.

Archaeopteryx: Magician?

Don't dis the archaeopteryx.
This old bird is good at tricks.
Mark my words, you look and listen:
she's a fairly skilled magician.
When she's huntin' or a fishin'
some poor critters, they go missin'.
Lizards slide into her throat.
Now you see 'em, now you . . .

James Carter

Ornithomimus

The fastest-running dinosaur,
this creature was so quick, it
would regularly break the law
and get a speeding ticket.

Graham Denton

Actually, this poem is taking a bit of what's known as 'poetic licence'. There is no proof as to who was *the* very fastest dinosaur of all (and, as far as anyone knows, no Dinosaur Olympics were ever held to find out), though the fastest dinosaurs were probably the ornithomimids, toothless meat-eaters with long limbs that superficially resembled ostriches. These included ornithomimus, dromiceiomimus and gallimimus, among others, and were said to be capable of reaching speeds of up to thirty-eight miles per hour. Pretty nippy, eh?

Spot the Dinos

(*Haiku Riddles*)

1.

You'd better watch out!
Super-swooper's back in town
talons razor sharp . . .

2.

Bulky like a whale
with snake-like neck, pebble brain,
head up in the clouds . . .

3.

Rhinoceros-like;
a horrible three-horn-faced
vegetarian . . .

4.

Massive meat-eater;
tyrant king of the lizards –
the name says it all . . .

1 & 2 James Carter, 3 & 4 Graham Denton

1. pterodactyl, 2. brontosaurus,
3. triceratops, 4. tyrannosaurus rex

There's a Dinosaur Behind You!

There's a dinosaur behind you
and he's looking really mean
he's the most unpleasant dinosaur
that I have ever seen

There's a dinosaur behind you
I don't wish to cause alarm
but I think he's fairly hungry
and intends to do you harm

There's a dinosaur behind you
now he's getting very near
so you'd better get a move on
and be quick to disappear

There's a dinosaur behind you
oh he's almost at your back
I would recommend you run for it
he's ready to attack!

There's a dinosaur behind you
there's no time to hesitate
if you stay a moment longer
it'll surely be too late . . .

There's a dino . . . wait a moment
no there isn't any more
there's no dinosaur *behind* you –
you're inside the dinosaur!

(Well, don't say I didn't warn you!)

Graham Denton

What Am I?

(*A Colossal Kenning*)

A...

long-goner
super-stomper

swamp-swimmer
death-bringer

head-banger
jaw-snapper

teeth-gnasher
bone-basher

mighty-biter
fierce-fighter

tiny-brainer
comet-hater

past-dweller
fossil-fella

The biggest
ever carnivore,
I was of course . . .
a DINOSAUR!

James Carter
(with the infant class at Dorchester St Birinus CE Primary School)

25

Allosaurus

Allosaurus loved to pork out.
Allosaurus loved to munch.
Always had his knife and fork out –
life for him was one long lunch.
Allosaurus was voracious,
any time was time to eat,
with a stomach all too spacious
that he crammed with dino-meat.

Allosaurus liked a blowout,
he was such a greedy beast.
Every morning he would go out
searching for the nearest feast.
Allosaurus, what a gannet!
with a quite gigantic girth.
When he roamed around the planet
tremors really shook the earth.

Allosaurus, how he flourished,
scoffing everything in sight.
Never was he undernourished,
nothing quelled his appetite.
So he grew to be enormous
and he took an age to fill.
Dining with an Allosaurus?
Just make sure *he* pays the bill!

Graham Denton

Big H!

The haikusaurus

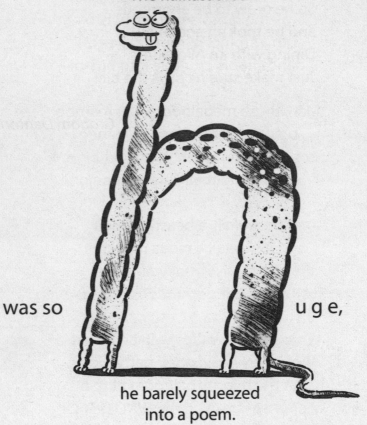

was so   u g e,

he barely squeezed
into a poem.

Graham Denton

NB: No relation to the cinquainodon or the tankalosaurus

The Dino Disco

From Zanzibar to San Francisco
all the raptors twirl 'n' twisto
to a stomp 'n' romp calypso
dance floors crumble into bits-o!

Man, those megalodons can mambo
boy, those brontos truly tango
oh what fun when they fandango
strumming their Jurassic banjo!

Best of all, a beastly conga
claw-to-tail a mega monster
to a slinky, funky number
all that crashing sounds like thunder!

When those reptiles twirl and twist-o
how they heave their hefty hips-o
at the mighty ballroom blitz-o
come on down . . . the *DINO DISCO*!

James Carter

My Dinosaur Dining

My dinosaur dining
was such a disgrace,
he loved nothing better
than stuffing his face,
he'd guzzle and gobble
and swiftly dispatch
as much as he could
down his gigantic hatch.

My dinosaur dining
was most impolite,
to see how he feasted
was no pretty sight,
he'd polish off meals
and would eat like a horse,
demolishing course after
course after course.

My dinosaur dining
was ever so rude,
his manners were awful,
his etiquette crude,
he'd never eat slowly,
he'd overindulge,
he'd cram and he'd jam
till his belly would bulge.

My dinosaur's vanished –
my mother got tough,
she said he was banished –
enough was enough!
I dine with a brother now
much *less* refined . . .
I really do miss
how my dinosaur dined.

Graham Denton

Welcome to Jurassic Pork

Welcome to Jurassic Pork,
please step right on inside,
we cater for all carnivores,
our doors are open wide.
Although it isn't fancy fare
our food is always yummy –
a dinosaur knows what he likes
inside his giant tummy.

We've *barosaurus* burgers,
there's *europasaurus* pies,
apatosaurus pizzas
of a quite enormous size.
The *nanosaurus* crumble –
a dessert that can't be missed –
has a rich *triceratop*ping
that no dino can resist.

There's deep-fried *stegosaurus,*
there's *diplodocus* with chips,
with *omeisaurus* sauces
and assorted dino dips.
Our *supersaurus* soufflé
is a favourite of T-rex –
once on their plate they cannot wait
to get it down their necks!

For centuries this diner is
where dinosaurs have dined,
you'll find us most hospitable,
convivial and kind.
So come along and join the throng
we're keen to be your hosts . . .
for *human bean* – that's haute cuisine! –
and what we dream of most!

Graham Denton

Today's My Dinosaur's Birthday

Today's my dinosaur's birthday –
I didn't sleep last night;
I had a bad foreboding,
and woke up with a fright.
My heart has started racing,
my stomach's in a knot,
I'm full of trepidation,
my nerves are almost shot.

I'm permanently fretting,
my mood is one of dread;
forget the celebrations –
I'd rather stay in bed.
Oh, today's my dinosaur's birthday –
I'm *so* down in the dumps . . .
I promised that today I'd give
my dinosaur the *bumps*!

Graham Denton

Headbangers!

Seconds from extinct o'clock
Stegosaurus yells *'LET'S ROCK!'*
and every dino everywhere
strums guitars made out of air!

Kerrang! they go *Kerrack! Kerrung!*
headbanging has just begun!
How those lumpies stomp their feet
grooving to a monster beat!

Seconds from extinct o'clock
they're inventing *HEAVY* rock!

James Carter

if...

dinosaurs were real, then maybe
dragons were as well. And perhaps
one day soon they'll find a skeleton
beside a cliff, inside a cave:
a backbone, a tail, a massive head,
and those branch-like bones
where the wings would have been;
or even a whole beast, perfectly
preserved in Siberian snow:
grey-green and scaly, those two top
canine fangs just jutting over the jaw,
the raging fire of the beast long lost
to the deep sleep of the dead,
those saggy eyelids closed
forever.

James Carter

Here's Looking Achoo, Kid!

Whenever a dinosaur
catches a cold
he's inclined to be
terribly sneezy.

Then ever so tight to your
hat you should hold –
cos it's certain to
turn very breezy!

Graham Denton

My T-rex Is Poorly

My T-rex is poorly,
my T-rex is ill,
he's really not feeling too great.

He's under the weather
and doesn't look clever –
it must be *somebody* he ate!

Graham Denton

Wanted:
One Dinosaur!

O woe is me!
O woe is me!
I'm totally
dismayed:

I want a dino
for my sis . . .
but nobody
will trade!

Graham Denton

Hop It! or ...
Footie Boy Finds T-rex!

I don't know why I ever bothered
turning up at the park for footie
every Saturday morning
as they'd always say
the same thing –
not to go near the ball,
not to touch the ball,
not to look at the ball,
not to even *think* about the ball.

So there wasn't much to do.
For ninety minutes.
So I'd get daydreaming about stuff.
Dinosaurs, mainly. And I'd go
up to our goalie and say something like,
'Hey, how many T-rexes d'you reckon it would take
to fill a footie pitch?'
And the goalie would say,
'*What?* Is that a stupid joke or something? HOP IT!'
Or I'd go up to him and say,
'Hey, what if there was a T-rex skeleton
right underneath this pitch?' And he'd say,
'*What?* Are you completely mad or something?
HOP IT!'

But in my head there would be
a real T-rex skeleton, waiting
in the thick mud below. And in my head
I'd be the one who dug the skeleton up,
all on my own, and I'd be a mini-celebrity
on the front page of every newspaper:
FOOTIE BOY FINDS T-REX!
And there'd be a big photo of little me
standing right next to the massive dino skeleton.
And then that goalie would come over,
look at my T-rex and say,
'Hey, is that some stupid dinosaur or something?'
And I'd say, 'HOP IT!'

James Carter

Palaeontologist

(pay-lee-on-tologist)

It's a tricky word to say –
it's a harder job to do
to dig around in dirt and mud
and rain and snow, though you –

would need to be quite patient
them dino bones are rare
and fragile too, and worth so much
so need a lot of care –

plus cleaning up and measuring
I think you get the gist –
when I grow up I'd love to be
a . . . palaeontologist!

James Carter

Frozen in time

Over millions of years

Snapshots of an ancient age

Skeletons held

In Earth's hard depths

Like nature's long-kept

Secrets

Graham Denton

Dinah D

Dinah D: a dino-bore?
Knows *every* type of dinosaur.
Its Latin name. Its height. Its weight.
Its habitat. And what it ate.

The Town Museum, working late:
Dinah's on a dino date!
Is she really such a bore?
Dinah – no, we think you're . . .
                              GRRRRRREAT!

James Carter

What Scientists Have Concluded from the Fact That So Many Plant-eating Dinosaurs Were of the Extra-large, Oversized, Super, Bumper, Jumbo, Giant, Mega, Massive, Vast Variety

Eating shrubbery
leaves you blubbery.

Graham Denton

Lizard

Little lizard
did you know
your ancestors
lived long ago?

They were bigger
stronger too
reptiles, yes,
but not like you . . .

No bugs for them
or flicky tongues
by hunting food
they had their fun

Of all the dinos
you're what's left . . .
to tell the truth
I like you best!

James Carter

Studying Dinosaurs

To examine the habits and features
of these most antiquated of creatures
you don't have to look
in a history book . . .
you can learn by observing your teachers!

Graham Denton

Lullaby for a Woolly Mammoth

(To the tune of 'Twinkle, Twinkle' . . .)

Woolly
mammoth,
hear me sing . . .
! go to sleep you hairy thing!
! You   can snooze outside my
! door   . . . just as long as you don't
!   !   snore. Come on, Shaggy, shut
 !   your eyes,   now it's
                time for   beddy-byes!

James Carter

49

Do Woolly Mammoths Have Nits?

Of course they do, you silly!
AND moths AND flies AND fleas,
AND cockroaches AND giant wasps
AND several swarms of bees.

Now cruise down to the chemist
and choose a giant jar
of 'Crush-the-Critters-Hit-the-Nits'®
and then it's time to start –

to wash old Shnozzle with a hose
and shampoo him with care
and then apply a king-sized comb
(though gently) through his hair.

You do this once or twice a day,
with plenty rubs and scrubs,
for Fuzzy-Wuzzy must be rid
of nasty nitty bugs!

And when his coat's a flea-free zone
reward him with a treat:
a stinging-nettle sandwich or
a buttercup to eat!

James Carter

Talking Teeth

My dentist, Pete, has a real
mammoth-tooth fossil. He keeps it
in his cupboard. It cost him ten quid.
It's a molar, and an ugly, rusty, lump
of a thing, as big and as chunky
as a brick. The tooth's got
these deep ridges, just right
for grinding leaves and grasses.
It's one hundred thousand
years old, yet it doesn't have
a single filling.

Wish I was a woolly mammoth!

James Carter

A Tiny
Ode to the Sabretooth Tiger

Toothy kitty
we're all fans
of your groovy
goofy fangs!

James Carter

Don't Look Now

Don't look now but I think you'll find
there's a dragon at your shoulder

Don't look now but I think you'll find
that he's got his eyes on you

Don't look now but I think you'll find
that he's really not that friendly

Don't look now but I . . . Oops, too late!
(Now, what did I say NOT to do??!!)

Graham Denton

How to Build a Dragon

Take . . .
The cunning of a trickster
the cruelty of a storm
the loneliness of mountains
the shock of early dawn

The hunger of the winter
the shiver of a tomb
the madness and the strangeness
of the dark side of the moon

The blazing of the mighty sun
the anger of a king
the elegance and deadly dance
of eagles on the wing

Now find a cave to work in
a cauldron deep and strong
with care, mix these ingredients
and toil from dusk to dawn

And when you see that **dragon** rise
be **quick** – be out – just run
though you have made a **life** anew
yours may soon be **done** …

James Carter

I'm a Very Snappy Dragon

I'm a very snappy dragon
and I'm in a mood today,
so be wary when you're near me
and be careful what you say.
I'm irascible by nature,
I am prickly through and through,
I'll display my indignation
at whatever you might do.

I'm notoriously grumpy,
I'm particularly gruff,
I am permanently sulky,
I am always in a huff.
You'd be wise to pacify me,
I'm ferocious when annoyed,
I can morph into a monster
I'd advise you to avoid.

I am touchy, I am tetchy,
I am quick to throw a strop,
I possess a wicked temper,
I completely blow my top.
I lack any sense of humour,
you won't ever see me smile,
I'm a picture of resentment,
with a belly full of bile.

I'm malicious and I'm vicious,
and my disposition's fierce,
I've a tongue of dripping venom,
I have talons that'll pierce.
You ignore this at your peril
for I guarantee you'll pay –
I'm a very snappy dragon
and I'm in a mood today.

Graham Denton

Spell to Keep a Dragon Away

O, maker of misery
keeper of mystery
weaver of wizardry
dragon, be gone!

O, stealer of jewellery
master of cruelty
taunter of royalty
dragon, be gone!

O, dealer of slavery
hater of bravery
breather of flamery
dragon, be gone!

Go choke on your fires,
your dreams and desires . . .
to far and beyond
dragon, be . . . g o n e !

James Carter

What to Do If You're a Gentle, Friendly, Very Peace-loving Dragon and a Cocky, Wannabe Dragon-slayer Comes Knocking at Your Cave

Ignore
the door.

Graham Denton

wings as wi**D**e as ancient oceans

eyes of molten crystal ambe**R**

teeth as sh**A**rp as white shark's fins

tail of a mi**G**hty python

scales of g**O**rgeous golden green

jaws that ever hu**N**ger

breath stolen from the **S**un

James Carter

62

Do Excuse Me

'Do excuse me, when I beat you,'
said the dragon to the knight,
'if I choose then not to *eat* you,
for I have no appetite.

'I don't mean to seem ungrateful.
Please don't think I'm being rude . . .
I just can't face one more plateful
of such flavourless tinned food!'

Graham Denton

Stealing a Dragon's Egg

(in Seven Haikus)

It is easier
to steal the soul of the sun
than one dragon's egg.

Yet, if you are brave,
patient, alert and silent
you might just succeed.

Never touch the nest:
even a slight rustling sound
will wake the mother.

If there is a crack,
leave the cave immediately:
the egg is hatching.

Wait for a full moon:
enter the den, make your way
swiftly and barefoot.

Listen for breathing:
ideally steady snoring
from nesting dragon.

Only take the egg
if it is in easy reach.
Quick! Do not look back . . .

James Carter

The Tibetan Dragon

A dragon whose home is Tibet, he
likes to feast on that beast called the yeti.
And, as for a snack,
well, he's partial to yak,
with a side plate of wholemeal spaghetti.

Graham Denton

Dilly the Damsel's Recipe for Dragon Pie

ONE DEAD DRAGON
(check it's, like, totally dead first . . .)
CHILLI SAUCE (EXTRA hot)
200 tonnes of BLAZING RED HOT CHILLI PEPPERS
YE OLDE ENGLISHE MUSTARDE (tongue-burningly hot)
VINDALOO CURRY POWDER (as hot as hot gets)
PUFF (the Magic Dragon) PASTRY
800 gallons of SCORCHINGLY HOT BOILING WATER
ONE *VERY* LARGE COOKING POT
AN OPEN FIRE

COOKING INSTRUCTIONS . . .
Drop the dead dragon into the boiling water (try using
a crane). Bung in all the ingredients. Bring to the boil.
Simmer for ages and ages. Plaster pastry on top.
Pop in GIANT microwave.
Have a glass of water to hand
during the meal, just in case.

ENJOY!!!

James Carter

Derek the Dragon's Recipe for Damsel Pie

ONE DAMSEL
(dead or not, they taste great)

PASTRY
(you don't have to bother
with this, to be honest)

COOKING INSTRUCTIONS . . .
Breathe over the damsel until nicely crisp,
then scoff in one go!

James Carter

What's a Good Name for a Dragon?

What's a good name for a dragon?
Maybe Derek or Eric or John?
What about Daniel or even Nathaniel
or something as simple as Ron?

No, a dragon's name has to be *scary*:
a Fiery, a Fury, a Claw-ed;
a name to give princesses nightmares,
and make a knight lay down his sword.

Oh, I'd so like a name for my dragon
for I know that he has one for me –
depending how friendly he's feeling
I'm Breakfast or Dinner or Tea!

Graham Denton

Missing: DAISY

Anyone seen my D R A G O N ?

Scary, Scaly
Tall 'n' Taily
Daisy the Dreadful Dragon!

She's got bad breath.
A temper true.
Eats old ladies. (Children too.)

She breathes out fire.
She puffs out smoke.
She'll singe your hair. She'll make you choke.

Anyone seen my D R A G O N ...?

She soars about.
She seeks out food.
Makes loud noises. (Mainly rude.)

Yes, she's grumpy.
Yes, she's smelly.
Big Butt always blocks the telly.

Anyone seen my D R A G O N . . . ?

And she's beastly.
And a pest.
But I love her. (She's the best.)

Please send Daisy
back to me.
Treat her well. Or you'll be tea . . .

Anyone seen my *D R A G O N* . . . ?

James Carter

Komodo Dragon

Here be creatures
ten feet long
Here be beasts
immense and strong
Here be huge
and brawny tails
Here be skin
with brownish scales

Here be brutes
who overpower
Here be monsters
that devour
Here be jaws
with lethal bites
Here be giant
appetites

Here be kings
from days of old
Here be tales
the ancients told
Here be teeth
of dinosaurs
Here be feet
with razor claws

Here be foul
and fetid breath
Here be eyes
as cold as death
Here be legends
newly born
Here be dragons . . .
you've been warned!

Graham Denton

The world's largest living lizard , the Komodo dragon, or monitor
lizard, is found only on Komodo and its few smaller outlying
islands north of Australia. It probably never was more widely
distributed, although maps of ancient mariners had notations
of 'here be dragons' dotted throughout the islands of what are
now Malaysia and Indonesia. It was not until the early 1900s
that scientists confirmed the existence of these incredible giant
reptiles.

The Ancient Greeks . . .

knew a thing
   or two
         about m o n s t e r s.

From their minds
   their mouths
         their myths
came c r e a t u r e s
         that still haunt us
               taunt us
                     today.

Beware of the dog:
   the three-headed C e r b e r u s
         that guards the gates
               of the underworld.

Keep your eyes on the bull:
   with the body of a man
         he's as strong as he is tall
               the menacing M i n o t a u r.

It's rude to stare
    at M e d u s a
        with her snakes for hair
        one look alone
            will turn you to cold stone.

There's more besides
    and what's for sure
        they don't make b e a s t s
        like these any more.

James Carter

Guess Who?

Do come into my labyrinth,
see where I spend my days.
My home is most elaborate –
it's certain to a-*maze*.

You'll find I'm quite hospitable,
but generous I'm not,
for being quite despica-*bull*
I tend to CHARGE a lot.

I'd love you for my dinner date –
though I'm a meanie who
would put you on my dinner plate
and make a meal of *you*!

So do please take a step inside . . .
and have a guided tour,
for I will gladly be your guide –
I am The . . .

Graham Denton

A 'Minotaur' (Greek for 'Bull of Minos') is a creature from Greek
mythology. Half-man, half-bull, it was said to live at the heart of
a giant maze-like labyrinth, locked away by King Minos, who was
terrified of it. And who wouldn't have been? Every nine years King
Minos sacrificed children to the monster to keep it at bay. Yikes!
Eventually, a prince named Theseus, the son of King Aegeus of
Athens, slew the beast and, with the aid of a ball of thread (tied to
the door of the labyrinth), was able to escape the dreaded maze.
The Minotaur was no more! The children were saved! Phew!

Magnified

a *BILLION* times

a bug

becomes

a BEAST

you'll find.

Once a cutesy little critter,
tiny bug becomes a killer:
gruesome as that great Godzilla.

Down that microscope you'll see
freaks of nature, if you please.
Insects as monstrosities . . .

Now a thing significant –
bigger than an elephant.
A teensy-weensy worker *ant*!

Darkens nearly half the sky –
eagles flee when its nearby.
What a pretty *butterfly*!

You be careful where you step –
bigger than a footie net.
Spider spins a mega web!

Could be troublesome indeed –
when it starts its big stampede.
Creepy-crawly *millipede*!

Luckily, to human eyes,
minibeasts are so small fry.
Couldn't even hurt a . . . ?!

James Carter

Godzilla!

Like some beast from days of yore
Spoken of in ancient lore
Who's this mutant dinosaur?
Aaaaaarrrrrrgggggghhhhhh, it's Godzilla!

Dangerous from head to toe
Seeing off each deadly foe
Hey where did that city go???!!!
Aaaaaarrrrrrgggggghhhhhh, it's Godzilla!

Knocking over buildings he goes stomping
    down the street
Squashing all before him with his two
    enormous feet!

Stands a hundred metres high
Towering against the sky
Shooting lasers from his eyes
Aaaaaarrrrrrgggggghhhhhh, it's Godzilla!

Blasting out atomic breath
Guarantees an instant death
What a weapon to possess!
Aaaaaarrrrrrgggggghhhhhh, it's Godzilla!

He is not a monster that you'd ever want to meet
Godzilla is a killer who's impossible to beat!

So . . .

Best be getting on your way
You'll regret it if you stay
The last thing you'll ever say?
Aaaaaarrrrrrgggggghhhhhh, it's Godzilla!

Graham Denton

I Was Spooked

I thought I saw
a *dinosaur*
down there at the park
turned out to be
a broken branch
dangling in the dark

I thought I heard
a **monster** scream
somewhere out of sight
turned out to be
the wild wind
wailing in the night

I thought I watched
a ***dragon***'s fire
flame across the sky
turned out to be
the setting sun
blazing over high

I thought of other
scary stuff
but it was all untrue
I was spooked
by silly things . . .
perhaps you've had this too?

James Carter

The Swamp Thing

If you go down to the swamp tonight
you're sure of a mighty shock –
there'll be no gators, so I'm told
or even a creepy croc

Look beyond the mist, they say
to view the beastie true
The Swamp Thing, yes, they call him that
he eats young feasts like you . . .

Now if you hear a ghastly growl
and gruesome yells of pain
The Swamp Thing's on his nightly prowl
to catch his tasty prey

And I've heard say he's caked in slime
and ooze and more besides
old Swampy's ever hungry see
he's never satisfied

Beware take care when by the swamp
don't trek beyond that log
Rivet! Rivet! What's that sound?
So Swamp Thing's just a . . . *f r o g* ? ! ? ! ?

James Carter

Mythical Monsters

(Haiku Riddles)

1.

A three-headed hound?
Imagine all that barking,
the postman's ankles!

2.

Meet this gorgon's gaze?
Stare into those stony eyes?
I'd be petrified!

3.

So . . . is it a bull?
Or a man? Or a monster?
Actually, all three!

4.

Hey, check out my dreads . . .
nine deadly, hissing serpents!
My name? H_2O!

1 & 2 Graham Denton, 3 & 4 James Carter

1. Cerberus, 2. Medusa,
3. The Minotaur, 4. The Hydra

Two Basilisks

(A Love Poem)

A charming pair,
this *hisss* and her
were meant to be –
most s e r p e n t l y !

They tied the knot,
now, in a bind,
they're permanently
Valentwined!

Graham Denton

Ode to the Loch Ness Monster

Nessie, you're a mystery!
One camera-shy celebrity.
A legend lost to history.
Absent one eternity.

Come back for a day, maybe?

Nessie,
      where've you gone,
            matey?

James Carter